ENGLISH CHANNEL

London

Dover

Calais

Netherlands

Belgium

Germany

Luxembourg

DISCARD

France

Paris

Switzerland

Lyons

Italy

Avignon

Cannes

MEDITERRANEAN SEA

Julie Andrews Edwards

LITTLE BO
in FRANCE

THE FURTHER ADVENTURES
OF BONNIE BOADICEA

ILLUSTRATED BY Henry Cole

HYPERION BOOKS FOR CHILDREN
NEW YORK

Printed in the United States of America

This book is set in Deepedene 15/23.

The artwork for each picture was prepared using oil paint on paper.

First Edition

1 3 5 7 9 10 8 6 4 2

Library of Congress Cataloging-in-Publication Data

Edwards, Julie, 1935–

Little Bo in France: The further adventures of

Bonnie Boadicea / Julie Andrews Edwards; illustrated by Henry Cole.—1st ed.

p. cm.

Summary: A little cat and her owner travel through France in search of work,

finding great adventure and, finally, good fortune.

ISBN 0-7868-0658-3 (hc) — ISBN 0-7868-2540-5 (lib.)

[1. Cats—Fiction. 2. Travel—Fiction. 3. France—Fiction.]

I. Cole, Henry, 1955– ill. II. Title.

PZ7.E2563 Li 2002

[Fic]—dc21

2001039003

Visit www.hyperionchildrensbooks.com

CONTENTS

CHAPTER ONE

The Adventure Begins

"Bo, WE'RE GOING TO BEGIN a new adventure," Billy Bates announced one day. "It's time to take a gamble and see what fortune has in mind for us—which is easy to say, but hard to do when you're broke and desperately needing a job," he added ruefully.

He pulled out a large map and spread it across the table with a sweep of his hand.

His tiny cat, Bo, jumped up beside him, wanting to play. Billy laughed. "Move, little one—I can't see a thing. Now, I've heard there are good prospects for a sailor in the south of France. We're here . . . on the east coast of England. If we could get to Paris, here"—his finger traced a line—"then perhaps we could work our way down to the south."

He rubbed Bo's ears and gazed thoughtfully at the map. "What say, Bo? Shall we give it a try?"

Bo purred contentedly. She didn't mind where she went as long as she was with her beloved Billy.

It didn't take long to pack a few belongings into a duffel bag. Billy counted up what little money he had left, and, bright and early one morning, he tucked Bo securely inside his warm jacket, and the two friends set out on their journey.

Billy hitchhiked to the coast, took a ferry across the English Channel, accepted a ride from a friendly couple, and eventually met a truck driver, who, glad of companionship, drove them the last hundred kilometers to the beautiful, bustling city of Paris. They parted company as the afternoon sun was fading, and gray clouds threatened rain.

Billy gazed about him at the wide, straight avenues, the cascading fountains, the gilded statues, and the ornate lampposts.

"We're here, Bo. We're actually here. Now to find those lodgings that my pal Charlie told me about."

He consulted his map and set off once more as large drops of rain began to fall.

It was dusk by the time he and Bo found themselves on a cobbled street, in front of a shuttered building, paint peeling from its walls, with a sign hanging loosely from one hinge that read HÔTEL SYLVIE.

"I guess this is it," Billy said dubiously and pushed open a glass-paneled door.

There was such a strong smell in the hallway that Bo immediately sneezed. Billy recoiled at the odor of boiled vegetables, old

2

shoes, and dust, and wondered if fresh air ever entered the place.

Ahead of them was a shabby parlor, full of overstuffed furniture. A tiny office on one side had a telephone on the wall and a desk with a bell on it. After waiting a moment, Billy pressed the bell firmly, and it rang through the small hotel with a rattle like pebbles in a tin can.

There was the sound of frantic yapping, and a scruffy poodle, white with yellow-stained whiskers, dashed into the room.

The hackles on Bo's neck stood on end, and she dug her claws into Billy's sweater.

"It's okay, Bo. I've got you safe," he reassured her.

They heard the click of high heels on a wooden floor, and a middle-aged woman appeared. She was large, and her clothes seemed too tight. Her lips were painted bright red, and bracelets jangled on her wrists. She patted her hair and said, "*Allô, oui?*"

Billy started to speak, but the little dog was making so much noise that it was impossible to be heard.

The woman picked up the dog and clapped it smartly on the nose. "Fifi!" she admonished sternly. "*Un moment, monsieur.* Let me put Fifi away." She opened a door behind the office and dumped the wriggling dog inside. Billy glimpsed an unmade bed and a mess of clothes.

"*Alors,* I am Sylvie de Gauloise. What do you want?"

Billy hesitated. "Um—I was hoping you'd have a room to spare."

"For how long?" She opened a leather-bound ledger.

"I'm not exactly sure."

Inside Billy's jacket, Bo sneezed again, and Madame Sylvie looked up, startled.

"*Mon Dieu!* What was that?"

"Oh, that's just Bo, my little cat."

"*Un chat?* Ah—*non, non*—not possible. NO animals." She slammed the ledger shut.

4

Billy's heart sank.

"She's a very *good* cat and extremely small."

As Madame Sylvie began to protest, he lifted Bo from his jacket.

"See, here she is. She'd be no trouble, and I'd be completely responsible for her. Would you make an exception, madame? It's late, it's raining . . . and your hotel was *so* well recommended."

Madame Sylvie looked at him skeptically, then stretched out a hand and scratched Bo behind the ears with long red-lacquered fingernails.

"She *is* very—*petite*. Maybe I do have a place that is away from the other guests. Perhaps for an extra ten francs?"

Billy swallowed. "That would be wonderful."

She pulled a key from a drawer in the desk and led the way to a flight of stairs.

"You have been in Paris long?" she asked as they climbed.

"We arrived today," Billy replied, looking about him. Upstairs was even more uninviting than below.

Madame Sylvie showed him into a low-ceilinged room at the very top of the building. A grimy window revealed a blurred view of the Paris rooftops. There was an iron bed, a table with a dead plant on it, a tall lamp, and a rail on which to hang clothes.

"Is there a bathroom?" Billy inquired.

"But of course. Downstairs. If you want a hot bath, it will be five francs."

"What about something to eat?"

"*Non.* We have coffee and croissants in the morning only."

"I see." Billy sat down on the iron bed, and the springs creaked and sagged beneath him.

Bo jumped onto the floor. She touched Madame Sylvie's shoes

7

with a velvet paw and brushed affectionately against her ankles, then sat and gazed up at her with unblinking, violet-colored eyes.

Madame Sylvie smiled for the first time. "She always travels with you?"

"Bo's my lucky mascot," Billy explained. "She saved my life once. Where I go, she goes."

"Perhaps I could find a little milk for her—and cheese and bread for you. But the cat stays in the room. I don't want any trouble."

"You are very kind. I don't wish to impose."

"Pas de problème."

Later that evening, Billy lay in bed, with Bo curled up beside him. He gazed at the chipped plaster ceiling and listened to the sound of voices drifting up from below and the clanging and banging of the pipes in the wall.

"Gosh, Bo, I wonder if we did the right thing." He sighed. "Well, at least we made it this far. We'll see what tomorrow brings." Bo licked his hand.

In spite of the fact that the room was too hot and the noise from the wet traffic below never ceased, they were both asleep within minutes.

CHAPTER TWO

The Trouble with Fifi

BILLY WOKE TO A DEAFENING SOUND and a feeling that the entire room was shaking.

A church bell nearby was striking the hour. Bo shot up so quickly that she almost tumbled off the bed. She burrowed beneath the threadbare coverlet.

Billy sighed and stretched and tried unsuccessfully to go back to sleep. Eventually, he took Bo in his arms and rose to open the dusty window.

They were greeted by a beautiful, fresh morning. Clouds scudded across the sun, and the tiled Paris rooftops stretched in front of them for miles. On a hill in the distance sat a beautiful, white domed building.

"Why, Bo—that's a famous church, the Sacré-Coeur," Billy said delightedly.

There was a noise at the door. Billy set Bo on the bed and crossed to open it.

Fifi streaked into the room, yapping furiously. Bo attempted to climb the wall, and Billy deftly caught the dog as she was about to leap on the covers.

"No, you don't, you rascal. Aren't you a terror!"

He turned and was startled to see Madame Sylvie wearing an embroidered purple kimono, her hair still sleep disturbed and in curlers.

"*Je m'excuse,*" she wheezed as she retrieved the snarling Fifi. "You see what happens when we have *les animaux* in the building! We did not sleep all night, and she escaped my room the moment I opened the door."

"No harm done," Billy assured her.

"I'm making coffee. You wish for some?"

"Thank you. I would also like to take a bath, and I must make a phone call."

"Use the telephone in the hall downstairs. It will cost five francs."

She seemed in no hurry to leave.

"You have plans, now that you are in Paris?" she asked.

"I'm hoping to find a job," Billy explained. "I'm a sailor, and I'm keen to travel. We're heading for the south of France."

Madame Sylvie looked at him thoughtfully.

"Well, I could use a young man in the hotel. Let me know if you are interested."

Billy gulped at the thought of staying one second longer than necessary in the Hôtel Sylvie, but said nothing. He trudged downstairs and took a bath in an enameled tub filled with rust-tinged water and returned to the attic, carrying a tin tray with a pot of coffee on it, a croissant, and some more milk for Bo.

"Well, my Bonnie. Here's a bit of luck. I telephoned a friend of Charlie's, Mademoiselle Liselotte. Isn't that a pretty name? She's offered to show me Paris later today."

He poured himself some coffee and choked as the strong liquid hit his stomach. "We're going to the Eiffel Tower and that white church we saw on the hill. And we'll dine at Le Club Hepcat."

He pulled on his clothes and checked his wallet. Then he lifted Bo and gazed into her eyes.

"You must be hungry, little one. I'll bring you back a nice, warm supper. Be a good girl while I try to find a job. Wish me luck." He kissed her nose.

Bo was horrified. Billy was actually going to leave without her. She bounded after him as he opened the door, but he gently nudged her back into the room. "You'll be much safer here." He smiled. She made another dash across the wooden floor, but he closed the door firmly behind him and Bo skidded into it and banged her nose. She sat down, her ears ringing, feeling

14

extremely bad tempered. Then, as she always did when annoyed, she began to wash herself.

Where I go, little Bo goes, Billy had said. *She's my lucky mascot.* If she was his lucky charm, then why wasn't she by his side at this moment?

Bo stretched, then wandered moodily around the room. She peered into the urn that held the dead plant and tried the remains of the coffee, but shuddered at the acid taste. She jumped onto the bed and deliberately kneaded her claws into the soft fabric.

She crossed to the door and listened. There was no sound from the other side. She listlessly tapped at the hem of the tablecloth. It had little tassels, which swung enticingly. Lying on her side, she grasped them and pulled herself along. There was an odd noise, and she thrust her head into the darkness beneath the table.

For one heart-stopping moment she was unable to breathe. Fifi was staring at her with blazing, angry eyes.

"Surprised you, little cat, didn't I?" she growled. "Thought you were safe, didn't you?"

Fifi lunged, and Bo clawed her way straight up the tablecloth, knocking the coffeepot onto the floor where it smashed into tiny pieces. She stared wide-eyed as Fifi put her nose between her paws and let loose a stream of abusive language.

"*Out, out, out!*" she yapped furiously. "Who said you could come here?"

Bo arched her back and tried several times to find her voice, but all that came out was a little squeak. She remembered the special name her father had given her, to help in times of fear. *I am Boadicea . . . I am Boadicea,* she reminded herself. And finally she managed to say, "There's no need to make such a *fuss.*"

"Are you leaving, or do I have to come and get you?" The dog growled impatiently.

Bo's eyes narrowed. "Why don't you just try?" she challenged.

Fifi looked surprised. Then, with an outraged snarl, she sprang at the table, and the chase was on.

Round and round the room they went, scrabbling on the carpet, sliding on the floor, streaking over the bed, and pulling down the pillows and coverlet. For one scary moment, Bo thought she was trapped; but she pretended to go left, then ran right, while Fifi continued straight on and crashed into the wall.

Bo tore across the room, ears flat against her head, and leaped up onto the windowsill.

"Had enough?" she asked cheekily.

Fifi backed away in order to see better, and toppled the lamp behind her. "I can easily get up there," she panted.

Bo pressed back against the window, not realizing that it was still unlatched. It swung wide with a crash, and she went tumbling out onto the roof, rolling over and over until she found herself clinging to the edge of a gutter and staring down into the street below.

For the longest moment Bo hung over the

precipice, swinging gently. From her view, people looked as small as ants, and the cars and bicycles resembled miniature toys.

"HELP!" she meowed at the top of her lungs. Frantically scrambling to gain a foothold, she clambered back up, but in her effort she dislodged a tile. It slid to the edge and fell down, down, down. There was a faint tinkling sound as it shattered on the pavement.

Inside the hotel, Fifi continued to bark—hoarse but triumphant.

CHAPTER THREE

The Reunion

BO SHOOK HERSELF SEVERAL TIMES to dismiss the irritating dog from her mind and looked about her.

The gutter was wide enough to make a little path. She padded along it carefully, making sure not to look down into the street, for that made her dizzy.

A pigeon panicked at the sight of her and noisily flapped away. Watching it, Bo did not see the big drainpipe.

She tumbled once more, this time into a black, gaping hole, and suddenly she was hurtling downward at a tremendous speed, swinging first one way, then another, emitting a little cry of surprise every time she changed direction.

She was just beginning to enjoy the ride when she exploded from the pipe into the sunshine and found herself lying on the cobblestones, dazedly gazing up at the rooftops where she had been only seconds before.

Bo waited for her head to clear. Then, picking herself up, she cleaned her whiskers and decided to go exploring.

From the roof, the city had seemed a pleasant place. At street level, it was a busy, blaring metropolis. Cars, buses, and bicycles swept by, horns honking, bells tinkling. Children were yelling and playing. Pedestrians were in such a hurry that they never saw the little cat, and she was almost trampled underfoot.

Darting into a passageway, Bo followed it and came to a tranquil, sunny courtyard. A tantalizing smell of freshly baked bread wafted from the open door of a cheerful-looking café shaded by an awning.

Sitting on a whitewashed step was a large, lustrous black cat. Bo hesitated, wondering if perhaps she could slip by without disturbing it. But the skin on the back of her neck began to prickle— a sure sign that something was strange. There was an aura about the cat, a familiar quality that made her heart suddenly beat faster.

The black cat opened its eyes and saw Bo. It yawned, sat up, and looked away, then suddenly sat up even taller and looked at her again. Its golden eyes fixed on her for the longest moment; then it said in a low and disbelieving voice, "Bo? Is that you?"

With a sudden thrill of pleasure, Bo realized why the big cat had so intrigued her.

It was her brother Tubs.

She ran to him, and the two cats greeted each other, nuzzling noses and purring their delight.

Tubs was saying, "*Ooh-la-la!* Holy mackerel! I thought I was dreaming. Of all the cats in the world, I never expected to see you, Bo."

"What are you doing here?" Bo gasped. "The last time I saw you, we had been sent to the pet store and a nasty man came and carried you off."

Tubs shuddered. "A terrible time. Remember how scared we all were? I ended up with the worst family. The children teased me and pulled my tail. I hardly ate at all. I lost so much weight, I looked like a skeleton's shadow."

"You look well enough now," Bo commented.

"Naturally, I ran away," explained Tubs. "I couldn't stay there. I dragged myself into a café, and the owner, Monsieur Peluche, took me in. He's my family now, the best friend a fellow could have, and a wonderful chef. We came to Paris and he started this restaurant. But enough about me. I want to hear about you."

Bo related all that had happened to her since that fateful day by the river when she and her brothers and sisters had escaped. She told how Billy Bates had found her, and how he had saved her from the dreadful storm and taken her aboard his fishing boat,

Red Betsy. She described her adventures at sea and their arrival in Paris and explained about Billy's needing to find a job.

Tubs said, "What a crackerjack story! I wonder what happened to the others—to Samson and Polly and Maximillian? I wonder if they ever found a home for themselves?" He sighed, then said abruptly, "Are you hungry?"

Bo was starving.

"Come with me," Tubs said grandly, and led the way up the steps of the café and into a bright kitchen.

Bo had never smelled so many wonderful aromas in her life. People were bustling about, cleaning and slicing food, cooking and stirring great copper pots on the stoves.

Tubs marched up to a dapper gentleman who was busy giving orders to everyone.

Tubs explained, "This is Édouard Peluche, my master. Watch this."

He meowed plaintively, and the man stopped talking and looked down.

"Ah, my friend. Time for your lunch, *n'est-ce pas?*"

Monsieur Peluche noticed Bo and smiled expansively. "What have we here? You brought me a customer, *non?* Such a pretty little flower. Well, you shall *both* have something to eat."

He clapped his hands at a young boy who was peeling potatoes. "Quick, Louis! Some *bouillabaisse pour les enfants, s'il vous plaît.*"

In a matter of moments, Bo was eating the most delicious fish stew. She and Tubs needed no encouragement to empty their dishes and leave them sparkling clean. Tubs licked the last particle from his whiskers, then burped discreetly.

"That hits the spot, huh? Now, Bo. What about letting me show you the sights of Paris? It's a grand city—the cat's whiskers."

Bo said excitedly, "Could I see the white church on the hill?"

"Le Sacré-Coeur? You may, indeed—*and* some other places along the way. I hope you're feeling energetic, for by the hair on grandfather's chin this is going to be a day to remember!"

Tubs bounded off, leading Bo back into the busy street.

"Stay close," he cautioned.

He indicated a small truck parked on the corner, filled with colorful spring flowers. "Goody! That's the ride we want. It travels all over the city. Come on."

The driver was climbing into his seat.

"Quick, Bo. Jump up!" Tubs leaped onto the back platform and tucked himself in beside some ferns.

Bo followed as the truck throbbed into life, and a moment later it lurched and moved out into the traffic.

"Isn't this just the ticket?" Tubs grinned.

Bo wedged herself between a big gardenia plant and a bowl of white lilies.

Tubs was yelling, "See that policeman in the middle of the road? He's called a *gendarme*."

Bo wondered how the gendarme managed to stay alive, for vehicles seemed to be coming at him from every direction. He had a whistle in his mouth, which he blew constantly.

"There's the Arc de Triomphe," Tubs shouted as they circled a huge stone monument with traffic buzzing around it like a whirling merry-go-round.

Tubs continued. "Terrific, isn't it? I fell in love with this city the moment I saw it. The food is great, and there's so much happening. If I live my nine lives over and over, I'll never tire of it."

The truck braked suddenly.

"There"—Tubs pointed—"the Eiffel Tower."

Bo gazed up—and up—and up—at the tallest structure she had ever seen. It soared skyward, seeming to touch the clouds.

Tubs said, "They say that from the top on a clear day you can see the edge of the world."

Bo looked about her, hoping to see Billy, but there was no sign of him.

"That's the river Seine," Tubs explained as they crossed a bridge spanning a wide body of water.

Racing through Paris, the truck climbed higher and higher, and the cobbled streets became narrower and steeper. Bo's fur was flattened by the wind, and the rough ride jangled every bone in her body. But she didn't mind. It was a thrill to be with Tubs, and his marvelous attitude toward life was infectious.

"Right, Bo. This is where we get off," he said as the vehicle crunched to a halt.

"Now what?" she asked, bounding after him.

"Follow me."

They were in a part of the city that was quaint like a village. Little shops sold antiques and secondhand books, chocolates, and souvenirs. Artists had set up easels and were painting and displaying their canvases. They had pictures to please everyone: landscapes, views of Paris, clowns, flowers, abstracts.

"These are my favorites." Tubs stopped beside a fine display of cat portraits.

"That one looks just like Mama!" Bo exclaimed.

"Mama's prettier. . . ." Tubs indicated a drawing of a lean, gray cat with a debonair charm. "That's Gaston, an acquaintance of mine. And this one—well, what do you think?" He nonchalantly struck a pose beside a large canvas of a resplendent black cat.

Bo gasped. "That looks *just* like you, Tubs."

"It *does*, doesn't it?

A group of tourists crossing the street noticed the cats and the cat portraits.

"These are good. Especially the one of this big, fluffy guy," said a man indicating Tubs. "Take a photo, quick."

There was the click of cameras, and several flashbulbs popped.

"Whoops. We'd better move on," warned Tubs.

They hurried away and came to a long, steep flight of steps.

"I often come here to visit a lady friend," puffed Tubs as they climbed. "She belongs to one of the priests at the church, and he feeds us very well. Now . . . I believe this is what you wanted to see."

Gleaming in the early evening light was the beautiful, white building Bo had glimpsed from the roof of Madame Sylvie's hotel: the Sacré-Coeur.

It was breathtaking, and so was the view of the city, for at that moment all the lights in Paris came on. They sparkled like jewels in the clear evening, and far, far away, the Eiffel Tower soared high over the rooftops.

Bo wondered if Papa had ever been here. He had traveled so much . . . perhaps he had once stood on these very steps.

After a moment, she said, "I wish I could find Billy."

"Where did he say he was going?" asked Tubs.

"He was coming here, to this church. Later he was going to a club."

"Did he mention a name?"

"It was something to do with a cat, I think."

"The Slinky Lynx?" asked Tubs, doubtfully.

"No."

"How about the Pink Panther?"

"No, no. It had 'cat' in the name."

"Hepcat. Le Club Hepcat?" Tubs brightened.

"That's it!" cried Bo excitedly.

"Hot dog! I know the place. Great for supper. What are we waiting for!"

CHAPTER FOUR

The Concert

Tubs WAS ALREADY HALFWAY down the street, and Bo ran to catch up with him.

"This part of Paris can be a little hair-raising," Tubs cautioned. "The felines around here are warmhearted, but there are a lot of tough guys, too."

Bo heard raucous voices and pulsing music. Neon signs flashed gaudy colors. She glimpsed frail cats, fancy cats, scrawny cats, cats lurking in doorways and skulking behind garbage cans. An undernourished pack of beggarly mongrels raced by.

Tubs led her through a maze of narrow lanes and alleyways, then turned off into a pretty square. Trees formed an overhead canopy, and fairy lights twinkled in the branches. Someone was playing a trumpet, and the music was slow and sweet. Below street level Bo glimpsed a large cellar packed with people. A sign read Le Club Hepcat.

Suddenly, she saw Billy.

"Look, Tubs! He's here. Billy's here. Come and see."

Billy was moving onto the dance floor with a young woman.

"He looks like a *fine* fellow, Bo. But leave him be," Tubs advised as she moved to go inside. "He wouldn't be pleased to see you."

"*Yes, he would!*" Bo said emphatically.

"Possibly. But then *our* fun would be over, for he would surely keep you with him, and we couldn't spend time together."

Bo thought about this, and his words made sense. With a wistful glance at Billy, she allowed Tubs to lead her farther along the street where the open door of the club's kitchen spilled light onto the pavement.

Inside, it was steamy and busy. Waiters yelled to one another over the noise of crockery and glasses being washed and stacked.

A thin-featured man with dark hair came to the doorway. He took a deep breath of the evening air and spotted the two cats.

"Hallo, Tubs. Haven't seen you in a while. Did Monsieur Peluche send you over here for a good meal?" He laughed sardonically, and the laughter became a racking cough. He disappeared, and a moment later returned with some scraps of food on a tin platter.

Tubs and Bo ate every morsel.

"A banquet for the soul," Tubs declared. "My whiskers! I feel ready for anything!"

He had no sooner spoken than four large, disreputable-looking cats emerged from the shadows. At the sight of Bo, they stopped, sniffing the air suspiciously.

"Er, Tubs . . ." Bo nudged him anxiously.

Tubs wheeled around, the fur on his neck bristling. Then he suddenly rolled over and said, "Hey, guys. I was hoping you'd show up. Bo, allow me to introduce the scurviest scoundrels this side of the catacombs."

He crossed over to a ferocious-looking white cat with large tan markings and a black patch over one eye.

"This is Big Jules. The meanest mouser in town."

"Hi, lady." The cat looked down bashfully and shifted restlessly from paw to paw.

"This rollicking rogue is Théophile." Tubs indicated a tall, mangy tabby with a bent and ragged ear. "He belongs to the club here. Théo—my sister, Bo."

Théophile purred. "Zowee, Tubs! Where have you been hiding this fabulous feline?"

Tubs continued. "Prosper here is a sweet sinner with a voice that could melt treacle off a tart."

A plain brown cat with large, limpid eyes bowed extravagantly.

Recognizing the fourth cat, Bo said shyly, "You must be Gaston. I saw your picture today."

Gaston fluffed out his gray tail appreciatively. "Any relative of Tubs is a friend of mine."

"So what's new, boys?" demanded Tubs.

Big Jules shrugged. "Not much. The neighborhood's been quiet."

"I had a catcall from Bruiser," Gaston remarked. "I told him we weren't interested in joining his flea-ridden pack."

Prosper said moodily, "Suzy's had kittens again."

The trumpet player in the club began a different theme: a jaunty, swinging tune.

"He's new," Théophile explained.

"He's good!" Gaston tapped a paw rhythmically.

"He sure is. Mmm . . . That gets me right here!" Prosper said as he scratched fiercely behind his ear. "Excuse me—I gotta wail."

He began quietly at first; then, warming to the music, he put his head back and yowled.

Gaston paraded back and forth, strumming the iron railing with his tail. He, too, began to croon. "Purrrrrfect!" he enthused as the music became more insistent.

Big Jules began to hum in a deep, rumbling bass, and encouraged by the lively trumpet, all four cats suddenly performed a marvelous, impromptu concert.

Prosper did indeed have a mellifluous voice. Théophile jumped onto a garbage can, kneading it with his claws and beating time. Gaston,

cool and debonair, strutted and swayed, winding himself about Bo so smoothly that she found herself swept up in the dance.

Tubs swished his tail in time to the music. "This is more fun than a mouse in a saucer of cream," he declared happily.

Two waiters came out of the kitchen to see what the noise was about, and, as the song ended with a flourish, they gave the cats a round of applause. Tourists who were leaving the club came over to see what was so entertaining.

"Time to be getting out of here," Tubs warned.

Bo's eyes were shining.

"Billy wasn't the only one to go dancing tonight. I had such fun—thank you."

Big Jules was suddenly shy. "Aww. Any time, m'mselle. Any time."

Gaston said genuinely, "Great to make your acquaintance, Miss Bo."

More people began to collect, and the crowd pushed forward.

Tubs said urgently, "Come *on*, Boadicea. We have to run."

They hurried out of the square just as Billy and his friend,

Mademoiselle Liselotte, emerged onto the street.

Billy caught a brief glimpse of Bo and stopped in his tracks. He called in disbelief. "Bo? BO? It *is* Bo! Hey, Bonnie."

He raced after her to the corner, but she had vanished.

"How very odd, Liselotte," he said as she joined him. "I could have sworn that I just saw my little cat."

"*Mais ce n'est pas possible!*" She laughed.

"Oh, of course—she's at the hotel. But the likeness was amazing."

CHAPTER FIVE

The Barge

BO AND TUBS JUMPED onto the back of a passing road sweeper. It was moving leisurely through the city, spraying water into the gutters and whisking them clean with large, round brushes.

Tubs said, "I suppose I should get home or Monsieur Peluche will be worried about me. And I wouldn't want to miss breakfast. But I know a good spot to find a little refreshment before we say good night."

They leaped off the truck as it neared one of the bridges, and Tubs walked with Bo down to the river and along the towpath.

Moored at the water's edge was a narrow, wooden barge. On her prow the name *Alouette* gleamed gold in the moonlight.

A man was sitting on the deck, smoking a pipe and gazing up at the stars.

Tubs meowed, and the man looked over and smiled. "Ah, I was wondering if you'd come by, *mon ami*. But there are two of you, I see."

He climbed down, bringing them a saucer of bread and milk.

"What a rascal you are, my little tomcat." He had a warm, gruff voice. "Next, you will bring the entire neighborhood."

Bo was feeling very full, so Tubs ate most of the snack while the friendly barge keeper made a fuss over her.

"We mustn't stay, Bo," advised Tubs. "It's getting really late."

A couple emerged from the darkness, strolling arm in arm, as Bo and Tubs scampered away.

Billy was saying, "It was a grand evening, Liselotte, and I do thank you. Now if only I had found a job today. . . ." He stopped, then said in a perplexed voice, "I think I must be dreaming, or Paris has me a little overwhelmed. Did you just see those two cats?"

"More cats?" Liselotte asked. "I don't see any. Today has been confusing for you, I think."

Billy walked over to the barge keeper who was picking up Tubs's saucer.

"Excuse me, sir, did you see two cats here a moment ago?"

"Oui."

"Was one gray, with a little white heart on her chest?"

"It is dark, my friend. But she was gray." The man smiled at Liselotte. "Allô, chérie. You haven't been to visit me in a while."

"You know each other?" Billy asked.

Liselotte explained, "Oh, everyone knows Georges. He's a

48

famous character on the river." She gave him a brief hug. "Georges, this is a friend from England, Billy Bates."

Georges offered his hand. "*Un plaisir.* You have lost a cat?"

"Yes. No!" Billy put a hand to his forehead. "I have a little kitten, but she is in my hotel room. I'm sorry. I just arrived in Paris."

"You are on vacation?"

"No. Yes. I'm sort of passing through."

Billy haltingly explained how he was on his way to the south of France and looking for a job.

Liselotte said, "Georges, you must know someone. Can't you help?"

Georges puffed on his pipe.

"You say you are a sailor?"

"Yes, sir. I was first mate on a herring boat."

"You have a long journey ahead. If you're not in a hurry you could go part of the way by *péniche.*"

"Excuse me?"

"*Péniche.* Barge. I could use an extra hand. I have a full load of gravel that has to be delivered near Lyons. I could take you as far as there. I leave tomorrow."

"I—oh—*gosh!*" Billy was overwhelmed. "That would be incredible. Are you sure?"

"I can't offer you much. Some food. A bunk to sleep in. My wife is away at the moment, visiting her mother."

Billy could not believe his luck.

"It sounds great," he said.

"Good. Then you have a job."

Georges laughed good-naturedly as Liselotte kissed him on the cheek. "Bring your things in the morning, Billy, and I'll show you the ropes," he said.

Tubs escorted Bo back to the Hôtel Sylvie.

She spotted the drainpipe that had been the beginning of such a wonderful adventure.

"I'm sad to say good-bye, Tubs. I've had such a lovely time."

"Me, too. A bang-up, dandy day." He touched her nose. "Come and see me again soon, Bo, now that you know where to find me."

"I will, I promise. I'm glad you're happy and have a good home."

Bo watched the big cat as he sauntered away, flicking his tail in a last farewell. Just like Papa used to do, she thought.

She turned her attention to the hotel. How was she to get back in? What if Fifi attacked her again? There was a definite possibility that the dreadful dog would be on the lookout.

She drew herself up and said firmly, "I am Boadicea."

A woman came along the street and entered the hotel. Bo slipped in after her and raced up the stairs. The attic door was ajar, and she flew into the room and crouched in the farthest corner, under the bed. There was no sign of Fifi.

Moments later, she heard Madame Sylvie's agitated voice and the sound of hurried footsteps.

"I am in shock, Monsieur Bates, to tell you what happened. I am afraid your little cat has gone."

"What do you mean—*gone?*" Billy sounded terribly anxious. "Calm down, madame. Please start at the beginning."

"First of all, Fifi was gone. I searched all over the hotel, and then I heard her barking in your room. When I opened the door, Fifi was there alone—there was no little cat. The window was wide open. I think perhaps she fell out. She was not on the roof."

"Oh, my Lord!" Billy felt his stomach tighten, and he ran into the bedroom and over to the window.

"Bo!" he cried into the night.

Bo emerged sleepily from under the bed and meowed.

"Why, here she is. She's *here!*" Billy scooped her up and hugged

her with relief. "Oh, I thought I had lost you."

Madame Sylvie placed a hand on her ample bosom.

"That is *incroyable*," she gasped breathlessly. "I tell you she was not in the room. I looked everywhere."

She sank onto the bed with relief, and the springs sagged beneath her with a loud *ping*.

"This is a *terrible* bed!" she said absently.

"Bo is so small, madame. I'm sure she was under the covers or something. The main thing is, she's here now." Billy stroked the little cat. "Did Fifi give you a bad time, my Bonnie? What a brave girl. What a good Bo."

"Excuse me for the confusion," said Madame Sylvie. "I will bring some milk and biscuits."

Billy yawned. "I had the best time, Bonnie. I saw all the sights of beautiful, fabulous Paris. The Eiffel Tower. The Sacré-Coeur. And guess what? I even found a job. Tomorrow we'll be on our way again. How lucky can a fellow get?"

But Bo never heard him. She was fast asleep in his arms.

CHAPTER SIX

The River

THE FOLLOWING MORNING Billy paid his bill, said good-bye to Madame Sylvie and an agitated Fifi, and with Bo on his shoulder, walked to the great river to find the barge once again.

Georges was sitting on the grass, reading a newspaper.

"*Bonjour,*" he called out. "I have something to show you."

He pointed to Bo.

"There's a picture of your little cat in my newspaper."

"Excuse me?" Billy was confused.

"She is here on the front page."

"Oh, you must be mistaken. . . ." Billy laughed.

"Then she has a sister, *non?*" Georges thrust the newspaper into Billy's hand.

There was a photograph of two cats standing by a collection of paintings—one of them resembling Bo in every detail.

Billy gasped. "This cat—with the white heart—is *just* like her. But who is the other cat? The big black one?"

"I think I may know this fellow." Georges tapped the paper.

"These are possibly the cats you saw last night."

"But it certainly wasn't Bo. She was in my hotel room, as I said."

"Are you sure?" Georges chuckled.

Billy looked perplexed. "This is remark- able. I'd like to keep this picture, if I may."

Georges rubbed Bo's ears. "I like cats. I have a stray on board at the moment. Come, I'll show you around."

He clambered onto the barge, and Billy picked up his duffel bag and followed.

Bo jumped onto the deck and stretched. The smell of brine and tar and sun-baked wood tickled her nostrils, and she felt happy and instantly at home.

Billy and Georges entered the pilothouse, and Bo padded to the far end of the barge and jumped down to a small lower deck. She gazed at the two huge anchors and the water below, her fur ruffled by the breeze from the river. It felt grand to be on a boat again, though this was certainly an unusual one. She settled into a com- fortable spot to wait for Billy and would have dozed, had it not been for a slight sound above her head.

Bo looked up and her eyes widened. Perched on the branch of an overhanging tree was a handsome ginger cat. It stared at her with such intensity that she felt quite self-conscious.

56

"*Bonjour, chérie.*" His voice was low and friendly.

Before she could draw a breath, he was on the deck beside her.

There was an air about him, a roguish charm. The markings on his face were distinct and handsome. His eyes shone like burnished copper pennies. He had a white, fluffy cravat of fur under his chin, and he carried his full, curving tail proudly, like a banner.

"What a treat!" he exclaimed. "We never get visitors like you on board. Where do you come from? What's your name?"

He moved closer. "*Mon Dieu!* I don't believe those dazzlers."

Bo backed away, drawing herself up as tall as she could.

"Excuse me," she said timidly. "I'd like some room, if you don't mind."

But that was as far as she got, for the bold cat was now only an inch from her nose, too close for comfort. She suddenly lifted her paw and cuffed him across the cheek.

"Ow!" He sat down abruptly. After a moment he rubbed his

face and said "Ow" once more, this time in a tone of respect. "What did you do that for? I was just being friendly."

"Well, I don't feel *that* friendly," replied Bo.

She squeezed past him and moved farther along the deck.

The cat bounded after her.

"Oh, phooey," he said. "Let's start again. I didn't mean to make you mad."

He ran around her.

"*Écoute!* Stop a moment and tell me who you are and why you're on my barge?"

Bo paused. "*Your* barge?"

"*Mais oui.* At least it is for the moment." He leaped onto a hatch.

"Panache is my name—adventure is my game. I'm a direct descendant of Moustafa the Magnificent. He was my great-great-great—well, never mind. It's enough to say that he was a *great*-great-grandfather."

He executed a quick turn. "*Maintenant,* tell me everything."

Bo considered for a moment. He was an impudent fellow, yet he did seem genuinely interested.

Keeping a proper distance between them, she told Panache all about herself and Billy, and how they happened to be in France.

When she had finished, Panache said slowly, "*Fan—tas—tique!* And now that you are here, will you stay?"

"I don't know," replied Bo. "It depends on Billy."

Panache yawned. "This is not a bad life. The barge is comfortable, and Georges and his wife are pleasant. It's a little slow. But now that you're here . . ."

He looked up as Georges and Billy appeared.

"Ah, you two have already introduced yourselves." Georges wagged a finger at Panache. "I hope you have been behaving."

He lifted Bo and whispered in her ear. "Watch out for this *gallant*. He has an eye for the ladies. Not that I blame him." He winked at Billy.

The days that followed filled Billy and Bo with wonder. They journeyed down the Seine and saw the magnificent cathedral of

Notre Dame, its ancient rose-colored windows reflecting the sun. They slid beneath bridges and cruised past exquisite waterside mansions, country cottages, and gardens.

They ate at little waterside cafés and visited local markets for supplies.

The river changed heights many times, and great locks enabled the barge to travel from one level to another. Each lock had huge gates at both ends. The first set allowed the barge into the lock. When the gates were shut, the water was lowered—or raised—bringing the boat in line with the next stretch of the river. At this point, the second set of gates opened and the barge continued on its way.

The two men and the cats traveled by day and moored along the water's edge at night. The men enjoyed each other's company. Billy learned how Georges and his wife lived on the waterways, bringing whatever cargo they could on their journey south, and when returning north, buying olive oils, mustards, jams, honeys, cheeses, sausages, and wine, which they sold at a big fair in Paris.

Bo and Panache were not getting along. Panache was certainly full of charm, but Bo was often annoyed by his breezy manner and his bouncy athletics. He was always dashing somewhere, or, when onshore, scrambling up trees and clinging to the underside of branches. Bo had the feeling that he was performing to impress her. Sometimes it was amusing, but most of the time she walked away from the ginger cat and found a quiet spot where she could observe what was happening with Billy.

Panache was not used to being ignored and would retreat to a quiet corner of his own and sulk.

CHAPTER SEVEN

The Peacock

ONE DAY BILLY CALLED to the pilothouse, "Georges, there's a big weir ahead. A lot of traffic, too, going through the lock."

"I see it," Georges replied. "We'll wait here, I think."

He slowed the barge to a halt, and the men tied it firmly to iron stakes, which they hammered into the riverbank.

"*Zut!* It will be a long while before we are on the other side," Georges said irritably. "Billy, run on ahead. There's a small store up there. You could pick up the things we need while we have time."

"Aye-aye, sir."

Billy carried Bo onto the towpath.

"Come on, Bonnie. Time for us to stretch our legs."

Panache was on the cabin roof. Seeing Billy and Bo walk away, he decided to follow, glad of some action.

The lockkeeper's cottage and garden were a sight to behold.

Flowers grew in profusion, radiant with color, and an immaculate lawn extended to the very edge of the water. A flagpole carried the French *tricolore*, which flapped lazily in the breeze.

There was a sandy area with swings and slides, where children were playing. A lady, with a baby in a carriage, was sitting on a bench, chatting with another woman.

The store was doing a brisk trade, and when the customers saw Bo, they exclaimed delightedly; but she didn't like the attention. While Billy waited in line, she wandered a little distance to explore.

There were chickens, busily pecking for scraps behind a fence, and a rabbit in a wire-mesh pen. Bo had never seen a rabbit before and was fascinated. He had long, floppy ears that touched the ground, and he wrinkled his nose at her.

Bo asked, "Why are you shut up like that? Don't you want to be outside?"

"*Non, non,*" he exclaimed. "That would be dangerous. I'd be stolen, or foxes would catch me. It's safer here. Besides, there's the peacock."

Bo had no idea what he was talking about, but she knew that she could never, *ever*, be penned up like that.

The lady with the carriage wheeled it over so that her little girl could see the rabbit, too, but the baby was more interested in Bo.

"*Pfleuh-si-fond-si-pouille-pfleuh,*" she gurgled, and dropped a springy cord with a yellow rubber duck on the end of it. It made a squeaky sound as it bounced up and down.

Bo tapped at it, and the baby laughed with delight. The mother reached out to touch Bo, but Bo darted away.

There was a small vegetable patch with beanpoles in neat rows, and winter cabbages growing amidst pansies and herbs. The warm earth smelled fresh and tantalizing. Bo was just about to sniff a clump of basil when there was a deafening shriek behind her. She spun around, hugging the ground in fear.

Confronting her was the biggest bird she had ever seen. It was a magnificent blue and green, with a beautiful crown of feathers and a long trailing tail.

It jabbed at Bo with a sharp beak, and she cried out in pain.

"You do NOT touch the garden!" screamed the bird, dancing in front of her. "Private property. Do you hear? PRIVATE."

It pecked her harshly once again, and again Bo gave a cry.

There was a clatter of beanpoles, and Panache was suddenly at her side.

"HEY, *mon vieux*! How about picking on someone your own size?"

The creature extended its glittering turquoise neck.

"You are addressing ME? Do you KNOW to whom you are SPEAKING?"

"I know you are a bully. I suggest you leave the lady alone."

The huge bird fluffed and puffed itself up and suddenly spread its tail, like a fan, displaying a wondrous rainbow of colored feathers.

"I am *Pruneau de Pompierre*, Prince among Peacocks. And YOU . . . are not welcome."

He leaned down to stab at Panache, but the brave cat lifted a paw and swatted the bird with unfurled claws.

This time it was the peacock's turn to cry out, and it shrieked several times with surprise and indignation.

The hens set up a racket. Children yelled and pointed at the sight of the peacock's spectacular tail. People stopped what they were doing. Customers ran from the shop to see what was going on, and the lady with the carriage stood up to get a better view.

Panache nudged Bo, and she scampered away from the hysterical peacock. The carriage with the baby began to free-wheel across the lawn toward the lock, gathering speed as it rolled. The

rubber duck was dragged, bouncing and squeaking, behind it.

Bo leaped after the little toy, and Panache was right behind her.

Billy, leaving the store, his arms filled with groceries, had a clear view of the runaway baby carriage.

Sensing the terrible danger, he dropped his bags and dashed to get to it before it reached the water's edge.

Bo and Panache pounced on the toy duck. The cord was pulled taut, jolting the carriage just enough to alter its course by a fraction. It missed the lock with inches to spare, and ended up in Billy's

outstretched hands. He took hold of it firmly, easing it to a halt.

The baby was gurgling with delight. Her mother raced across the lawn, scooped the child up and hugged her, sobbing with relief.

Billy grabbed Bo, and Panache streaked back along the towpath.

The peacock was still screaming his lungs out in the background, but no one paid any attention.

Billy told Georges all about it.

"*Mon Dieu*," Georges said. "That's truly *incroyable*. You mean our two cats actually helped save the baby?"

"They really did," said Billy. "Everyone was amazed. I believe Bo knew what she was doing."

He stroked her. "Well done, my Bonnie," he whispered. "You're amazing."

She licked his nose and purred.

Later, she went looking for Panache and found him in his favorite spot on the pilothouse roof.

"*Bonsoir, ma petite.*" His eyes sparkled. "Are you feeling better?"

"Much better. I came to thank you for what you did."

"Ah, we had some fun, *non*? A little action for a change."

"You were very brave," Bo said shyly.

"Oh, *la!* I never liked that crazy bird. He got what he deserved."

They looked at each other for a long moment.

"Don't go," Panache said. "Stay awhile. It's pleasant out here."

Bo hesitated. Then she moved to sit quietly at Panache's side, and the two cats gazed into the starry night.

CHAPTER EIGHT

The Mistral

THE JOURNEY SOUTH CONTINUED, each magical day yielding to another as the barge wound its way down the river, making a wide V as it pushed through the water.

They passed through tunnels cut deep into the cliffs. Georges used a powerful searchlight to guide the vessel as they floated through the eerie shadows and listened to the *plop-plop* of moisture dripping from the walls.

In the evenings, cattle appeared ghostly white in the misty fields, still as statues, and the night creatures sang their special songs.

Billy sighed contentedly. "This is better than being on *Red Betsy* in rough seas, eh, Bo? Isn't this much nicer than having old Cap'n Svenson yelling at us?"

Bo agreed wholeheartedly.

Early one sparkling morning, Billy noticed a group of men searching the undergrowth near the water's edge.

"What are they looking for, Georges? Mushrooms?" he asked.

"Snails," replied Georges, lighting his pipe.

"Excuse me?"

"*Mais oui.* They are a great delicacy in France."

"You eat *snails?*" Billy was aghast.

Georges laughed. "And frogs' legs, too."

"Oh, *yuck!* I could *never* do that."

"But you did. Last night."

"*What?* I thought we were eating chicken!" Billy clutched his stomach.

Georges grinned wickedly. "We're having chocolate ants for dessert this evening."

Billy put his hands over his ears.

But he had to laugh.

As they approached the suburbs of Lyons, Georges spread out Billy's big map of France.

"You might try looking for a job in Cannes." Georges indicated the port with a stab of his finger. "The harbor's full of grand yachts. During the spring they start preparing them for summer travel and usually take on extra crew. It's a bit early, but you might get lucky."

"I'm going to have to find something soon," said Billy. "My money's almost gone."

"Then perhaps a train to Avignon and across country by bus. With good connections you could be in Cannes by nightfall. Though buses are rather unpredictable," Georges warned, "and there's the mistral."

"The mistral?" Billy asked.

"The wind from the north. It can be cruel. You'll know when it comes."

Panache said to Bo, "It's going to be boring around here. Maybe I'll move on as well."

"Where will you go?" Bo asked.

"Wherever my fancy takes me. I always land on my paws. Perhaps we'll meet again sometime, *non?*"

"I would like that," Bo said.

"Hmm. You'll probably miss me dreadfully."

Bo thought he sounded just like Papa.

With Billy's help, Georges unloaded his cargo, and suddenly it was time to say good-bye. Georges's wife was arriving on the afternoon train, and Georges offered to take Billy to the station.

Billy packed his duffel bag and glanced one last time around the now familiar barge.

"We've had a good time, haven't we, Bonnie?"

He picked her up and resolutely joined Georges on the dock.

"*Au revoir, chérie,*" Panache called from the roof of the pilothouse. He was looking forlorn, and Bo thought that, in spite of his bravado, he really was a good fellow at heart.

At the railway station, Georges pressed a bag of sandwiches and fruit into Billy's hands.

"To keep the wolf from the door—at least for a day," he grinned. "Stay in touch."

"I will," Billy vowed, and the two men embraced.

"Look after the little one," Georges called as the train began to move. "If she ever wants a good home, you know where to send her!"

"Not a chance!" Billy yelled. "Thanks again for everything." He waved until Georges was out of sight.

The train gathered speed, and they passed through beautifully manicured countryside: vineyards with row upon row of young grapes, orchards of peaches, cherries, and apples, bursting with early spring blossom. They crossed and recrossed the powerful, ever-widening river, which thrust its way toward the sea. In the far distance, the mountains were topped with snow. Above the tallest hung a gray-black cloud.

Hours later Billy and Bo sat outside the tourist office in Avignon, waiting for their first bus and eating Georges's

sandwiches. Billy leaned against the wall, enjoying the warmth of the sun, and looked about him at the imposing medieval town. Life was good, he thought.

Bo lifted her head, and her nose twitched at the new scents of pine and eucalyptus on the fresh spring air . . . and another scent that she couldn't define. The skin on the back of her neck began to prickle. Something didn't feel right.

Their first bus took them several miles into the countryside and deposited them at a crossroads where they were to make another connection. Fields of young lavender plants and poppies surrounded them, and there was not a soul in sight. According to Billy's map he was exactly where he was meant to be, but he began to wonder if the bus driver had understood his questions or perhaps he hadn't understood the bus driver and read his timetable correctly.

A dull roar began nearby, sounding as if a great body of water were coming their way, but within seconds the poppies were flattened by a fierce, blustery wind. Swirls of dust danced about Billy's feet, and his jacket seemed to take on a life of its own as it strained to be free.

Bo had been walking to stretch her legs. She was bowled along the road like tumbleweed, and as she struggled to reach Billy, she was, in fact, carried in the opposite direction.

Billy was propelled forward by the wind and was able to reach her and scoop her up. But when he tried to return to the bus shelter, it felt as if he were pushing a great boulder ahead of him. He staggered back under cover and tucked Bo inside his jacket.

He wound a scarf about his neck, turned up his coat collar, and stamped his feet. No matter which way he faced, the gusting wind bit and pulled and whipped at him. There was no sign of traffic, and he supposed that even if there had been a bus, it would have probably been forced to pull off the road.

"My word, Bo. This must be the mistral that Georges was talking about."

Hours passed, and the temperature dropped. Bo became chilled and crept up to nuzzle at Billy's neck, and each gave the other warmth to some degree. As the light faded and evening settled, Billy hunched down beside his duffel bag, the only protection between him and the elements.

"Looks like we're here for the night, Bo. What I wouldn't give for some food and a hot cup of tea. Let's just pray that someone comes by before we freeze."

As if in answer, two dots of light appeared in the

distance, and Billy made out the shape of a ram-
shackle bus lumbering and swaying toward him.

Excitedly, he ran into the road, waving his arms and shouting,
and the vehicle jolted to a halt with a squeal of brakes. Billy flung
his bag aboard and stumbled up the steps, grateful to be free of
the icy wind.

A round of applause greeted his entrance. Billy blew on his
frozen fingers and glanced around.

Eleven passengers were smiling at him, and all started speaking in French.

A woman at the very back sat next to a wire cage containing
two live chickens. Several children carried schoolbooks and were

teasing and jostling one another. A dark-haired man wore several strings of onions around his neck. A portly friar held a wide basket covered with a cloth on his ample lap. The bus driver, toothless and lined with age, looked as though he should have retired many years before. The heat generated by the bodies on board made the interior seem deliciously warm. As the bus lurched into action again, Billy was flung into a vacant seat.

He lifted Bo from his jacket, and there was a chorus of *oohs* and *aahs* at the sight of her, and another round of applause.

Maybe it was the little cat or the fact that Billy looked so exhausted, but a woman offered her shawl, the children gathered

around him, and the friar whipped the cloth off his basket, revealing bread and cheeses, which he handed out to everyone.

As the old bus fought to stay on the road, slewing, sliding, slowing, or accelerating at the whim of the buffeting mistral, everyone was grateful for the others' company, since to be alone on such a night would have been scary indeed.

It was very late when they reached the port of Cannes. Still the storm raged. Billy stumbled down several damp and wind-chilled streets until he came upon a youth hostel. He took a room for the night, threw off his jacket and shoes, and fell onto the bed, with Bo at his side, to sleep nine hours without waking.

CHAPTER NINE

The *Legend*

THE MISTRAL HAD BLOWN itself out by morning. When Billy and Bo emerged from the hostel, silvery sunlight was flooding the town, and fluffy clouds hung like cotton balls over the hills and mountains beyond. A warm breeze carried perfumes of pine, flowers, brine, and seaweed. Flags fluttered and palm trees swayed, their long leaves making a rustling sound as they touched.

Billy said, "This is definitely the place for us, Bo. But we've only money for bus fare and one meal, and then we're really in trouble. I must find a job by the end of the day."

He walked to the harbor where he found a marine agent's office. Setting Bo on a window ledge inside, he crossed to a desk to make inquiries. Bo basked in the warmth of the sun and looked out at the gleaming yachts. They were moored in neat lines, straining at their hawsers and bobbing gently in the water like a vast armada anxious to put to sea. Tiny dinghies *putt-putted* about the marina, their outboard engines sending blue haze into the clear air.

Bo wondered if Papa had ever visited this place. Surely, he must have, for it was wonderfully interesting.

Billy returned, looking disheartened.

"No luck, Bo. I've been advised to try some of the other ports. So we'd better be on our way."

They journeyed from town to town and harbor to harbor, each place prettier than the last. Hotels, bars, and cafés along the shore sported gay awnings that shaded chairs and tables. Villas in colors of terra-cotta, pink, and mauve dotted the hillsides, festooned with balconies and flowers. People wore bright clothes, and music came from every side. Cars sped along the sea road, and motorbikes dodged and weaved around each other, their engines buzzing like angry hornets.

By late afternoon Billy had covered many miles. He was footsore and dejected. Although he had made inquiries all along the coast, there was no job to be had, not even the promise of one.

He sank onto a bench and gazed at the blue-and-green sea, where a boat with a white triangle of sail was tacking back and forth, heading for harbor and home.

"I guess it's too early in the season for anyone to hire new help." He sighed. "What happens now is in the hands of the fates, for I really don't know what to do next."

Bo's tummy rumbled. She meowed and climbed onto Billy's shoulder to lick his face.

"Oh, Bo, I'm a fine fellow." He rubbed her chin. "Here I am, feeling sorry for myself and you're in need of food. I'm starving, too. What say we give it one more shot, then blow the last of our money on a decent meal?"

He walked resolutely down a winding hill toward a picturesque harbor. Beneath shady trees, a quaint restaurant advertised its menu on a big wooden board. A long, yellow stone breakwater sheltered several yachts. On the other side was a curving, sandy beach. Billy noticed a brown wooden ship with three tall masts and a raised deck at one end. It was called *Black Fin*.

"That's a Chinese junk," he said, his interest piqued. "I wonder how it got here? It's a long way from home."

A high-pitched shriek made Bo jump in alarm.

Sitting on one of the masts was a bright green parrot. It preened and ruffled its feathers, then it shrieked again and called in a raucous voice, "Belay there, landlubbers!"

A man's head appeared from a hatch on deck. He had red hair, a red beard, and a ring in his right ear. "What do you want?" he called.

"Nothing, sir. I was admiring your boat," replied Billy. "How does a Chinese junk end up in the Mediterranean?"

"Sailed her myself from Hong Kong."

The man climbed on deck and looked up at the sky, absent-mindedly scratching his belly.

The parrot cried, "Look sharp starboard!"

"Hush up, you scurvy, flea-ridden bag of feathers," the man yelled.

"No peace around here," he told Billy. "Can't sleep. But she's a good lookout, I'll say that."

The parrot screeched, "Clear the decks!"

"What's her name?" asked Billy, laughing.

"Alopecia," replied the man. "Mine's Jed. Cap'n Jed. Been here a long time. Came after the Second World War. What brings you to paradise?"

"I'm looking for a job. My name's Billy Bates."

"What kind of a job?"

"I'm hoping someone needs a first mate."

"You'll be lucky, laddie," Cap'n Jed replied. "You could ask the harbormaster, I guess. Miserable old salt . . . down at the end there."

"Aye-aye, sir. Many thanks," said Billy.

"Aye-aye, sir," echoed Alopecia.

Billy walked on toward the break-water. Fishermen mending their nets looked up and nodded a greeting. He touched his cap to them and strolled along the quay, stopping every now and then to admire the boats. There was *Cygnet* out of Marseilles, *Tempest* from Newport, *Breesea* out of Harwich, and *Mystique II* from Villefranche.

He came to a sudden halt. "Will you look at that!" Billy gasped in wonder and stared, transfixed, at a yacht moored directly ahead of him. "That's it, Bo. You'll never see anything prettier than that. My Lord, look at her lines."

He sat down on his duffel bag, his legs feeling weak.

The yacht was long, sleek, and superbly crafted, and exuded grace, strength, and elegance. Her decks were made of teak, her woodwork burnished a tawny mahogany brown, her chrome so

polished that it glinted in the afternoon sunlight. She had a high, gently curving prow and two incredibly tall masts that reached for the sky. A British flag fluttered off the aft deck, and on her transom the name *Legend* was embossed in large, golden letters.

Billy was mumbling, ". . . about a hundred feet of the trimmest motor-sailer I'll ever see. That's the yacht for us, Bo. One day . . ."

Bo heard the *clip-clop* of hooves. A tiny donkey weighed down by two panniers filled with colorful flowers was coming toward them. A friendly-looking man walked alongside him, making encouraging noises.

Billy got up to make room for them to pass, but they halted right in front of the *Legend*.

The man said cheerfully, *"Bonjour, bonjour!"* Then he called out, *"Mademoiselle Marie-Claire? C'est Monsieur Abelard avec les fleurs."*

A door to the main salon of the yacht flew open, and an enchantingly pretty girl emerged and hurried down the gangplank and onto the dock. She was barefoot but wore a white, soft-textured dress and her shining hair was caught at the nape of her neck with a bright

92

ribbon. She smiled at Monsieur Abelard and exchanged greetings with him in rapid French.

He placed large bunches of daffodils, tulips, and sweet-smelling hyacinths in her arms. Thanking him, she gave him money, then took some lumps of sugar from her pocket for the little donkey. Turning, she caught sight of Bo on Billy's shoulder. She gave a cry of delight and, hesitating only a moment, moved to caress her. Her hand was cool and gentle.

"*Ayiee—quel joli petit chat,*" she said in a lilting voice. "*Comment s'appelle-t-il?*" Looking into her clear blue eyes, Billy felt his heart turn over. Clasping her bunches of flowers, she was as lovely a picture as he had ever seen.

"Oh. Would you—I mean, do you—speak English?" he asked, feeling foolish.

"*Mais oui*—a leetle bit." Marie-Claire smiled. "What eez the name of your baby cat?"

"Um—Bonnie. But I call her Bo."

"She eez very . . . appealing."

Billy had an urge to reply, *And so are you.* He cleared his throat and said instead, "Do you live aboard this beautiful yacht?"

"Ah—sometimes." Marie-Claire smiled again. "I work for Sir Barnaby and Lady Goodlad. You have heard of them?"

"No, not at all." Billy wished he could appear a little more intelligent.

Marie-Claire stroked Bo. "They have this yacht. So, *oui*, I live on board, when they make a trip."

She waved as the flower man headed back along the dock.

"*Au revoir, Monsieur Abelard. Merci!*"

She looked at Billy for a moment, then said quietly, "Well—I have to go." But she didn't move. "You are looking for someone?" she asked, her eyes sparkling with humor.

Billy said, "Not exactly. I arrived today. I'm looking for a job.

I'm a first mate . . . but I'll soon have my captain's papers," he added quickly.

Marie-Claire nodded and rubbed one bare foot against the other.

"I'm about to visit the harbormaster," Billy explained. "I'm hoping he will know of something."

"*Monsieur Le Gros?* Oh, he went home an hour ago."

Billy's heart sank. There would be no more job opportunities that day.

Marie-Claire moved up the gangplank.

"Please—what is your name?" she asked.

"Billy Bates."

"Good luck, Billy Bates. You have a nice cat," she said shyly. "*Au revoir.*"

Billy watched her leave.

"*Au revoir,*" he whispered.

He let out his breath as if he had been holding it for a very long time.

"Phew! That's one special lady."

With a sudden resolve, Billy swung his duffel bag onto his free shoulder and said, "Come on, Bo, we've done all we can. Let's get something to eat before we drop."

CHAPTER TEN

The Goodlads

THEY WENT TO THE RESTAURANT by the
harbor. After studying the menu and the prices on the board outside, Billy said, "We'll see if the food in the south of France is as
good as they say," and pushed open the glass door.

Bo was instantly reminded of Monsieur Peluche's wonderful
kitchen in Paris. Delicious odors of garlic and warm bread, herbs
and spices tickled her nose.

There were several round tables, each with a soft pink cloth
and a glowing candle. The walls were hung with photographs.
At the back of the room, a white marble counter held a shining
machine with steaming pumps and levers.

Billy sniffed the air appreciatively.

"Cappuccino!" he declared happily.

He sat down at a table by the wall and placed Bo on the table
beside him.

A man wearing a blue-striped apron over his shirt and trousers came forward to take Billy's order. He had a long, sad face, and his hair was plastered down and parted in the middle. He introduced himself as Carlos, from Portugal.

Billy ordered a plate of fresh grilled sardines, a mixed salad, and a cappuccino. He was so hungry that he ate all the bread in front of him while he was waiting.

Bo looked around the room.

Near the window a young woman sat with a little boy who was talking animatedly and spooning a plate of soup.

An elegantly dressed man and woman were seated at a table on the far side. The man was robust with a ruddy complexion. The lady, blond and vivacious, appeared several years younger. They seemed to be having a marvelous time, for they laughed a lot and raised their glasses to toast each other.

Nearest to Bo and Billy, two men were seated by an alcove. They were an odd-looking pair, one swarthy and muscular, the other exceedingly thin, like a beanpole. They hardly spoke a word to each other but enthusiastically attacked two pink ice-cream sodas.

A jolly-looking man behind the counter sang along with a radio which was playing old French ballads. Near him lay a huge white cat. Bo thought she looked like Mama. Not as beautiful, not as fluffy, but with the same sweet expression in her eyes.

Billy's meal arrived, and he cut up three of his sardines, put them on a plate, and set them in front of Bo. She attacked them hungrily.

The elegant lady across the room caught sight of Bo and touched her companion's arm. He swiveled in his seat to get a better view, then said to Billy, "That's a delightful animal you have there."

"Thank you, sir." Billy smiled, wiping his mouth with his napkin.

The lady got up from the table and crossed the room.

"Forgive me, but I just adore cats."

She had a pleasant, cultured voice.

"Barney, come here a moment," she called. "Look at this tiny creature. Look at the color of her eyes. Would you mind if I held her a moment?" she asked Billy.

"Not at all," he replied.

The man smiled. "I hope we're not bothering you. Haven't seen you in town before. Just arrived?"

"Yes, sir. Last night."

"In the mistral? That was interesting, wasn't it? Good job we weren't at sea."

"You have a boat?" Billy inquired.

"We own the *Legend* here in the harbor."

Billy gasped.

"Then you must be Sir Barnaby. Oh, you have the most beautiful yacht I have ever seen."

Sir Barnaby glowed with pride.

"She *is* pretty, isn't she? We got her two years ago, in time to sail on our honeymoon. Today is our anniversary."

Billy offered his congratulations. He noticed that Lady Goodlad's eyes were almost the same color as Bo's and gallantly said so.

Sir Barnaby laughed.

"She used to be known as 'Jewel-Eyes Jessie'—one of the

famous Bluebell girls from the show in Paris. Many a stage-door Johnny tried to woo her."

Lady Goodlad blushed. "Oh, Barney!"

"But I won fair and square, didn't I, my love?"

She gazed at him adoringly. "You absolutely did, my dear."

Bo noticed that one of the two men nearby was talking on a phone in the alcove. She felt the familiar prickling at the back of her neck and wondered what could be wrong.

Sir Barnaby was saying, "Time to settle up, I suppose."

He called to the man behind the counter. "Delicious meal, Hilaire. As always."

The proprietor waved, and Carlos from Portugal brought the bill.

"I'll take mine too, please," said Billy, putting the last of his francs on the table.

He opened the door for Lord and Lady Goodlad, and they stepped out into the warm, sweet-scented night air. The lights around the harbor sent reflections dancing on the water.

Billy took a deep, contented breath and extended his hand to the Goodlads.

"It's been a pleasure to meet you both."

There was the roar of an accelerated engine as a huge black car suddenly hurtled around the corner and headed straight toward them. Its tires screeched as it came to a jarring halt.

The door was flung open. Before anyone could tell what was

happening, a man dressed in black with a dark hat and a kerchief jumped out and roughly took hold of Lady Goodlad. He began to hustle her toward the car.

She gasped and cried, "Barney!" in an alarmed voice.

Bo was still in Lady Goodlad's arms. She glimpsed the man's menacing eyes and sensed an evil that she would never forget.

Lady Goodlad cried out once more, and her high heels slipped on the edge of the curb. Sir Barnaby flung his arms about her.

A second man inside the car yelled, "Come on, *come on!*" and reached out to help his accomplice.

Billy acted instinctively. He dove for the bandit's knees, and with all his strength yanked the man's legs from beneath him. The bandit released his grip on Lady Goodlad, fell backward into the car, and hit his head.

Bo twisted herself free and landed heavily on the front of the vehicle.

"Let's go, *move* it!" the second man shouted to the driver.

The car's engine accelerated and whined, but the vehicle didn't pull away because the driver couldn't see where he was going. Bo was spread-eagled across the windshield, her mouth drawn open in a terrible grimace. Every hair on her body was standing on end, and she was yowling as if all the dogs in the world were tearing at her tail.

It took only a second for the driver to gather his wits, but that gave Billy time to help Sir Barnaby pull Lady Goodlad clear of the open door. The driver gunned the car's engine, roared off up the hill, and, cursing at little Bo, turned on the windshield wipers.

Bo was momentarily pinned to the car, but the wiper caught her little body and swept her into the gutter, where she rolled over and over like a rag doll caught in a tornado.

Lady Goodlad was sobbing. The proprietor of the restaurant rushed out with the waiter and the other two men. Everyone was talking at once.

"Are you all right?"

"*Mon Dieu*, what happened here?"

"Let's get inside."

"Carlos, fetch coffee at once."

Billy made sure the Goodlads were safely indoors, then looked around for Bo. She was nowhere to be seen.

"Bo," he cried in alarm. "Bo!"

He rushed along the street and spotted the tiny bundle lying in the gutter.

"Oh, my Lord!" With a terrible fear in his heart he picked her up very, very carefully.

Bo opened her eyes, hiccuped, and took a great gasp of air. Then she flung herself at Billy and burrowed inside his jacket.

Billy laughed with relief, his eyes brimming.

"It's okay, Bo. I've got you safe. No one can harm you now. What a brave girl. What a good Bonnie."

CHAPTER ELEVEN

Surprises

LADY GOODLAD, LOOKING PALE, was sipping a coffee. Her clothes were torn, and her knees badly scraped. Sir Barnaby sat with an arm around her, gently brushing the hair out of her eyes. He looked as shaken as his wife.

As Billy entered, Hilaire, the proprietor, announced, "Cognac for everyone," and Billy was handed a glass of golden liquid. He asked for warm milk for Bo and gently extracted her from his jacket and set her on the table.

Bo was dazed but miraculously unhurt. She lapped up the milk and felt it warming her stomach.

At the sight of her, Lady Goodlad stirred.

"Oh my, that poor kitten." She smiled wanly at Billy. "You both saved me from a terrible fate."

"They certainly did," Sir Barnaby concurred. "We owe you a lot, my lad."

The larger of the two men from the other table asked, "Do you have any idea why this happened?"

"Hard to tell," replied Sir Barnaby. "I doubt it was robbery, since they didn't take Jessie's purse. My guess is they probably wanted to hold her for ransom."

Lady Goodlad gasped. "You think so, Barney?"

"Looks like it, my love," her husband said grimly.

The thin man asked, "Did anyone get a look at the car or the license plate?"

"I think it was a Mercedes," said Billy.

But no one had spotted the license number.

Sir Barnaby helped his wife to her feet. He turned to Billy.

"Would you do me a great favor, young man, and walk with us to the yacht? I'd feel safer."

"Of course, sir."

"I'll get Jessie aboard; then I should report this to the authorities."

Billy gathered up Bo and, after thanking Hilaire for his hospitality, escorted the Goodlads toward the *Legend*.

Marie-Clarie and other crew members came running down the quay. Cap'n Jed rushed over to them, as did several other boat people.

Sir Barnaby pressed a piece of paper into Billy's hand.

"Here's my card, Billy. I'd like you to come and see me tomorrow morning if that's convenient."

Billy's heart skipped a beat. "Oh—yes, sir."

"Good. Let's say eleven o'clock? Our deepest thanks for your help tonight."

Billy waited until the Goodlads were safely aboard.

Cap'n Jed said worriedly, "I heard the commotion. What a terrible thing. I hope that's the end of it."

Billy said, "I'm sure they'll secure the yacht tonight."

"What about you, lad?"

"Me? Oh, I'm fine."

"No, I mean what are your plans now? Do you have a place to park your bones?"

"Um—actually, I don't," Billy replied.

"Then you'll stay on *Black Fin*," Cap'n Jed said generously. "I have a spare hammock. Come with me."

Later that night, Billy turned on his flashlight to look again at the card Sir Barnaby had given him.

It read,

The Lord Goodlad

NEPTUNE STEEL AND SHIPPING

GREAT BRITAIN

Bo pushed her nose above the blanket to gaze at Billy's face. He was lost in thought, and she meowed quietly. Billy touched her chin and rubbed her ears, and suddenly all the pent-up emotion of the past few hours was released.

"Oh, Bo," he took a deep breath. "What do you suppose

tonight was all about? Why would anyone want to hurt Lady Goodlad? And why does Sir Barnaby wish to see me tomorrow?"

Billy lay in the gently swinging hammock and reviewed the events of the day. Cap'n Jed's snores rumbled through the ship, and Alopecia muttered in her sleep. He heard the sea lapping at *Black Fin's* hull, the night sounds of the harbor, and the clanging of a buoy. He was still awake when a pale yellow dawn crept into the sky.

Billy presented himself at the gangplank of the *Legend* at exactly eleven o'clock. A handsome man in uniform was waiting to greet him.

"I'm Captain Ian Fraser," he said pleasantly, extending his hand. "The Goodlads are expecting you, if you'll follow me."

They moved aboard the superbly furnished main salon of the yacht.

Lady Goodlad was looking much better and offered Billy coffee and sweet rolls. She took Bo onto her lap.

Sir Barnaby said, "Billy—thank you again for your help last night. Jessie and I were very impressed. We were planning a cruise in about six weeks, but under the circumstances we feel we should leave as soon as possible. Captain Fraser will need an extra hand, and we've heard you're looking for a job. Would you be interested?"

Billy put down the cup and saucer he had been holding, for fear that his trembling hands would spill coffee all over the white carpet.

"Sir, I'd be more than interested," he managed to say. "I'd be delighted."

Lady Goodlad smiled. "Of course, the job is only on condition that Bo come with you."

"Bravo." Sir Barnaby beamed. "Bring your things aboard, Billy. You can start today. Captain Ian will fill you in on the details, and you'll meet Wally, our engineer, and Lucy, our cook. You've already met Marie-Claire, I believe. They're good people, and I think you'll get along."

An hour later, having told Cap'n Jed of his good fortune, and having collected his belongings from the *Black Fin*, Billy stood on the *Legend's* foredeck. With Bo in his arms, he inhaled great gulps of fresh air in an effort to calm his excitement.

"I don't believe it, Bo. What a break! What a wonder! A job—and on the yacht of my dreams. I'll be seeing lots of Marie-Claire as well. How about that! I do believe you've brought me luck once again."

He was so ecstatic that he squeezed Bo a little too hard. She whimpered, for she was still sore from the previous night's adventure.

"Sorry, Bo. That was thoughtless of me." He set her down gently.

Bo stretched. Knowing Billy was happy made her equally so. If only Papa, Mama, and Tubs could know of the wonderful things that were happening.

A bantering voice called to her from the breakwater.

"Bonjour, pussycat."

Bo looked up, startled.

Panache was sitting on the wall, looking wickedly pleased with himself.

Bo gasped with delight, then raced down the gang-plank onto the quay.

The ginger cat said airily, "Well, this *is* a surprise!"

"How did you know where to find me?" Bo asked.

"Find you? I had no idea you were here. I happened to be explor-ing the area."

"Oh, I see." Bo sat down.

"So—what delicious things have you been doing since last we met?" Panache brushed her chin with his tail.

Bo excitedly described her adventures since leaving Georges's barge: the terrible mistral, the long bus journey, and the frightening events of the previous evening.

"*Mon Dieu!* I leave you alone for two days and you are in trouble already. Obviously, you cannot manage without me."

Bo stood up, indignant. "Excuse me," she said. "I've been managing perfectly well."

"That's not what I heard," stated Panache. "There are rumors along the coast that you were nearly killed by a car."

Bo tipped her head. "I thought you didn't know I was here?"

"Yes, well—I didn't for a while." Panache was suddenly shamefaced. "Oh, phooey, let's not argue."

He leaped at a passing butterfly and narrowly missed falling off the edge of the quay.

"Panache, you silly. I am glad to see you," Bo laughed.

"Ha! Thought you might be." His burnished copper eyes gazed into hers. "Maybe I'll stick around for a while. I love adventure, and you seem to attract it wherever you go."

Leaning forward, he very gently touched her nose with his—and to Bo's surprise she didn't mind at all.

Glossary of French Terms and

Alors: Well, then

Alouette: Lark

Au revoir: Good-bye

Bonjour: Hello

Bonsoir, ma petite: Good evening, my little one

Bouillabaisse pour les enfants, s'il vous plait: Fish soup for the
  children, please

C'est Monsieur Abelard avec les fleurs: It's Mister Abelard
  with the flowers.

Chérie: Darling

Comment s'appelle-t-il?: What's his name?

Écoute: Listen

Fleurs de Paris: Flowers of Paris

Gallant: Naughty rascal

Incroyable: Incredible

Je m'excuse: Excuse me

Les animaux: Animals

Les Pêcheurs: Fishermen

Expressions

Maintenant: Now

Mais ce n'est pas possible: But it isn't possible.

Mais oui: But of course

Merci: Thank you

Mon ami: My friend

Mon Dieu: My God, or For heaven's sake

Monsieur Le Gros: Mister Le Gros

Mon vieux: Old buddy

N'est-ce pas?: Isn't that right?

Non: No

Oui: Yes

Pas de problème: No problem

Quel joli petit chat: What a pretty little cat

Un chat: A cat

Un moment, monsieur: One moment, sir

Un plaisir: A pleasure

Zut: Darn it

JULIE ANDREWS EDWARDS is a renowned figure in the world of entertainment. An exceptional vocalist, actress, and humanitarian, she is perhaps best known for her performances in *Mary Poppins*, *The Sound of Music*, and *Victor/Victoria*. She has received critical acclaim for her stunning performances on Broadway in *My Fair Lady* and *Camelot*.

She is also the author of several praised books for children, including the first in the Little Bo series, *Little Bo: The Story of Bonnie Boadicea*, and the *New York Times* best-selling Dumpy the Dump Truck™ series, a collaboration with Emma Walton Hamilton and Tony Walton.

HENRY COLE has created a new cast of *purr*-fectly whimsical characters for this sequel. He is the illustrator of many celebrated children's books, including *Bravo, Livingstone Mouse!* by Pamela Duncan Edwards; *Moosetache* and *Mooseltoe* by Margie Palatini; and his own *Jack's Garden*.

LITTLE BO'S
TRAVELS

by road
- - - - - - - -

by water
_____

by rail
|||||||||||||

ENGLIS
CHANNE

London

Dover

Calais

B

Paris

France

ATLANTIC OCEAN

Spain

Andorra

MEDITE